The Old Woman and the Jar of Uums

by jill Wright/Pictures by Glen Rounds

G. P. Putnam's Sons
New York

Text copyright © 1990 by jill Wright
Illustrations copyright © 1990 by Glen Rounds
All rights reserved. This book, or parts thereof,
may not be
reproduced in any form without permission
in writing from the publisher.
Published by G. P. Putnam's Sons, a division
of The Putnam & Grosset Group,
200 Madison Avenue, New York, NY 10016.
Published simultaneously in Canada.
Printed in Hong Kong by South China
Printing Co. (1988) Ltd.
Book design by Christy Hale.

Library of Congress Cataloging-in-Publication Data
Wright, Jill, 1942–
The old woman and the jar of uums.
Summary: A little old woman and naughty boy fall
under the spell of a magic jar, making them say
''Uumm,'' and must go to the hideous Willy Nilly
Man to get the charm lifted.
[1. Magic—Fiction. 2. Humorous stories] I. Rounds,
Glen, 1906–   ill. II. Title.
PZ7.W94940k 1990 [E] 88-29708
ISBN 0-399-21736-3

1 3 5 7 9 10 8 6 4 2
First Impression

Once upon a time in the woods, a little old woman was out pickin blackberries to make jam. Reachin for a specially juicy berry, she spied a funny-lookin jar. It was green glass with red and brown swirls and it was bent in the middle like somebody had kicked it.

"Pick me up," said the jar.

"This is a mighty friendly little jar," the old woman said. She picked it up. It looked to be empty. She shook it...nothin come out. She looked in it...nothin there. So she took it home, wiped it out, and filled it up with sugar.

Then she commenced to makin her jam. She set some black-berries to boil in her big old pot. "Pick me up," said the jar. She picked up the jar and put a shake of sugar into the jam.

Jest as she set the jar down, "Pick me up," it said agin, and she picked up the jar and put more and more sugar into the jam. Seemed like ever time she set the jar down it said "Pick me up," till she had poured all the sugar out of the jar into the jam.

PICK
ME
UP

"Why, this jam has twice as much sugar as regular jam," said the little old woman. She put her spoon into the bubblin pot and tasted it. "Uum," she said. "UUUmmm, that's fine."

The jam got ready, and she made her biscuits and set the table. She set it for two cause Jackie McPhee was on his way over. Jackie McPhee was the meanest, orneriest boy in the woods. He had fiery red hair and wild-lookin brown eyes and a streak of mischief in him that drove everbody crazy. "Rotten eggs!" he'd yell and then one would land on your porch. The little old woman was mighty tired of his tricks. She got his folks to send him over for tea and the biggest talkin-to of his life.

She knew when he got there because she heard "Rotten eggs!" and she poked her head out of the door and looked around.

"Rotten EEEGGGSSS!!" There was a smelly old rotten egg about to land on her porch, she was sure of it. She grabbed her broom and started shakin it.

"Don't...uum...DONT!"

"Aw, I was jest funnin you," said Jackie McPhee, steppin out from behind the bush where he'd been hidin. He was all dressed up in his Sunday best, his hair was slicked back, and he was clean as a whistle. Course, he'd brought some rotten eggs with him and a toad to put in the teapot, but she didn't know that.

"Uum, uum, come in and uum, uum, sit down," said the little old woman. Then she thought, "I don't generally stammer like this. What's the matter with me?" But she couldn't seem to stop sayin uum.

PICK
ME
UP

While the boy was gittin settled, she refilled the funny-lookin jar
with sugar and set it on the table.

Then she gave Jackie some sassafras tea. Soon as he had the cup
in his hand, "Pick me up!" said the funny-lookin jar.

Jackie was so surprised he dropped his toad to the floor, where
it went hoppin away. He picked up the jar and put a spoonful of
sugar in his tea. "UUUmmm," he said, "that's good."

Then the jar said "Pick me up!" agin.

Ever time Jackie thought he was through with the sugar, the jar

said "Pick me up," till he had 14 spoonfuls of sugar in his tea. Finally he set the jar down and it was quiet.

He started gulpin his tea and stuffin jammy biscuits in his mouth with both hands. Pretty soon, he asked the old woman if he could uum...uum...have another biscuit with jam. (He'd already had 4.) She said "Uum, uum, I reckon," and then she started to give him a talkin-to.

"Jack—ie Mc—Phee," she wanted to say. But all that come out was "Uummy Uum Uum!" She tried agin. "Rotten uums!" she said.

"Uum?" he said.

"Rotten UUMMMS!!"

The little old woman and Jackie McPhee stared at each other. Why was they both sayin uum?

To clear their throats, the little old woman poured them more and more tea and the funny-lookin jar said "Pick me up" lots more times, so they put all the sugar from the jar into their tea and drunk it down. The more they drunk, the uummier they got, till finally they was just uummin to each other and couldn't say no words atall.

"Uummy Uum Uum," said the old woman, gettin red in the face.

"Uummy Uum!" said Jackie McPhee, puttin down his teacup and lookin at the old woman like she'd poisoned him.

Something powerful strange was happenin. The old woman looked at Jackie McPhee. He looked at her. Then they both looked at the funny-lookin jar. "Pick me up," it said.

The old woman went over and picked it up. She turned it upside down. On the bottom was written a message:

> Caution: Hainted Uum Jar.
> Drinkin or eatin out of this here jar
> will make you say 'Uum.'
> P.S. It don't wear off.

They had been eatin sugar out of a magic uum jar all day long. No wonder they couldn't talk. She and Jackie McPhee were in big trouble.

The boy puckered up his face and looked like he was goin to cry. The old woman set down in the rockin chair and rocked herself back and forth. What was they gonna do? There must be somebody who could help em. Then it struck her. There was only one person in the world who could help. It was the Willy Nilly Man.

Now, if'n you don't know, the Willy Nilly Man is scairy. He got a beard that goes all the way down to his knees and spiders live in there and worms, and little blobs of grease and food he's eaten kinda hang all over it. And his eyes is scairy. One of em looks one way and the other one looks the other way so's you cain't tell exactly where he's lookin. He got one big long black tooth and he never washes hisself.

But he knows jest about all the magic there is to know. If'n anybody could stop the uums, it was him.

The old woman put on her shawl and tried to tell Jackie McPhee where they was goin.

"Uummy Uummy Uum!" she said pointing out the door, and meanin "Willy Nilly Man!"

"Uummy Uummy Uum!"

Jackie McPhee didn't understand what the little old woman was uummin about. If he had of understood, he would of flat refused to go. Jackie was mean and he was ornery, but like all children in the woods, there's one thing he was plumb scaired of and that's the

Willy Nilly Man. See, if'n the Willy Nilly Man don't like you, he can jest up and change you to a fat sow bug or a slimy old worm.

So it's probably jest as well the little old woman couldn't tell Jackie McPhee where they was goin. She started uummin at him. She uumed him out the door all right, but then she jest couldn't seem to git him movin. He was lookin mighty scaired and he kept tryin to run, and finally she had to grab him by the back of the collar, put him in her old wheelbarrow, and push him along.

Jest as they was leavin the house, "Pick me up" said the jar, and the little old woman picked it up and put it in the wheelbarrow on top of Jackie McPhee.

Jackie McPhee didn't like it in the wheelbarrow. They was a-bumpity bumpin through the woods so hard his teeth begun to rattle. Finally he got so upset he started to cry. The old woman stopped the wheelbarrow and put her red shawl on him to make him feel better. He quit cryin but he rolled hisself up in a little ball and snuggled on down under the shawl till she couldn't hardly even see him. She didn't know if this was good or bad, but she jest let him be, cause there, right in front of em, was the clearin where the Willy Nilly Man lived.

Now the Willy Nilly Man's house is scairy. It's all tacked up out of cardboard and tin cans and things what other folks don't want. There's a cow skull where most folks'd have a winder and trash heaped up where most folks'd have a garden. There's a couple of skinny old dogs slinkin around lookin mean.

But none of that was half as scairy as the Willy Nilly Man hisself. He was sittin in the middle of the clearin, beatin on his magic drum, singin "Dogs, scratch yourselves! Dogs, scratch yourselves!" And his old dogs was rollin round and round on the ground scritchin and scratchin till they like to scratch their own ears off.

That ain't the worst. After the dogs had a good scritch-scratch, the Willy Nilly Man beat his drum agin and sung "Jar, show yourself! Jar, show yourself!"

At first the little old woman thought maybe he was jest singin about any old jar but then that magic uum jar she had in her hand begun to itchin and tinglin. It didn't say "Pick me up" though, most likely cause she was already holdin it.

"Jar, show yourself! Jar, show yourself!" The Willy Nilly Man left off drummin. "Come here, you old uum jar. Where are you? I knowed you was here this mornin."

Course, what he didn't know, nor the old woman neither, was that the jar had said "Pick me up" to the dogs and one of em had picked it up in his mouth and carried it off to the bushes, where the old woman found it.

"Jar, show yourself!" The Willy Nilly Man started up his drummin agin.

The little old woman didn't know what to do. If she stepped forward with the jar, the Willy Nilly Man might be glad to help her cause she was the one bringing his jar back. On the other hand, what if the Willy Nilly Man was mad because she had his jar to begin with?

"Jar, show yourself!"

The old woman's hand that was holdin the jar jest kinda moved forward into the clearin by itself, and drug her along behind, pushin the wheelbarrow.

"Well, looky here," said the Willy Nilly Man. "See who brought my uum jar home to me! Where'd you git it, old woman?"

The little old woman didn't say nothin. She jest put the jar down on the ground and kinda backed up. How was she gonna ask him fer help?

"Pick me up," said the jar.

The Willy Nilly Man picked up the jar. "Well, old woman, speak up, I cain't hear you. Where'd you git it?"

The little old woman cleared her throat.

"Uum...Uum..." She wanted to explain but no words come out.

"So you bin USIN it, have you? Who said you could do THAT? And where'd you GIT IT?" he asked agin, real mad. "Did you STEAL IT?"

The Willy Nilly Man was standin right next to her now. She was close enough to see the spiders in his beard and the point on his tooth and she was pretty near petrified.

"You oughta know better than to steal from me! The onliest man to ever steal from me ended up as a crawdaddy with eyes stickin out on stalks and long scaly legs!"

The old woman tried to think of a way to explain to the Willy Nilly Man that she hadn't stolen his uum jar. She'd jest found it on the ground in the woods. She hadn't meant no harm by pickin it up. And anyways, how was she to know it belonged to him?

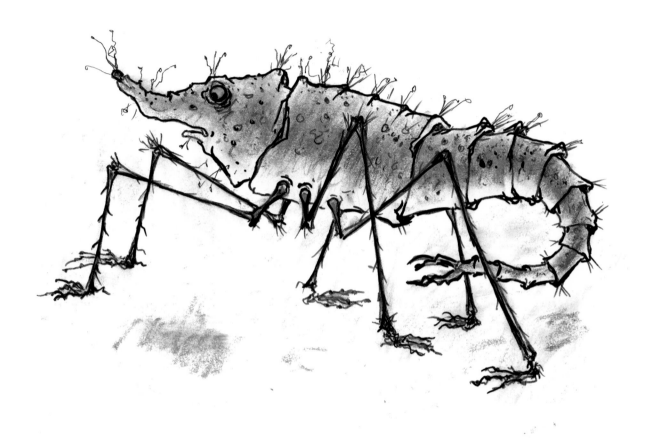

"This jar has got a powerful ju-ju magic on it," said the Willy Nilly Man. "Ain't nobody knows how to mess with ju-ju magic but me." He sat down at his drum agin. "Maybe I'll jest turn *you* into a crawdaddy! Serve you right for stealin my jar!" Now a crawdaddy, if'n you don't know, is a little crablike thing that lives in the river. It's the ugliest thing alive.

The Willy Nilly Man set to drummin. "Legs, stretch yourselves, legs stretch yourselves..." he sang at the old woman's legs, and she could feel her knees itchin to stretch theirselves out into craw-daddy legs and her feet tryin to git all scaly. She was so scaired, she hopped first on one foot and then the other. She kinda hoped the Willy Nilly Man wouldn't notice the wheelbarrow or Jackie McPhee all covered up by her red shawl. No use in both her and the boy turnin into crawdaddies.

Suddenly, out from under the shawl come a terrible sound!

"UUUUUU…" the shawl seemed to be moanin and wigglin around all by itself… "MMMMMMM!!!"

The Willy Nilly Man stopped drummin.

"What you got there?" he said, rollin his eyes.

Jest then, Jackie McPhee, still all covered up by the shawl, raised up a little and hollered "UUMMY UUUMMM!" meanin "ROTTEN EEEGGGSSS!" and he threw 2 rotten eggs at the Willy Nilly Man!

SPLOOSH! SPLOOSH! The stink was awful.

Now the Willy Nilly Man ain't like most folks. He don't mind rotten eggs theirselves. Fact, he eats em for breakfast ever mornin. But havin rotten eggs pitched at him from a moanin, wigglin shawl was jest too much.

"You got a magic ju-ju shawl!" he hollered. "How's I to know you had ju-ju magic too? Don't let that ju-ju shawl git me! Don't let it!" he yelled and he commenced to shakin in his shoes and backin away from the wheelbarrow.

"Pick me up," said the jar of uums, and the little old woman picked it up and shook it in the Willy Nilly Man's face. Seein him so scaired over a little boy covered by a shawl had give her back her gumption.

"Uummy Uummy Uum!" she shouted at him in her fiercest voice.

"All right, all right, old woman, don't make no never mind, you can have the jar, take it. Jest git that shawl thing outta here before it throws somethin else at me!"

"Uum?" said the old woman agin, meanin "How do I stop sayin uum?"

"Suck on a pine needle and then drink clean water outta the jar," said the Willy Nilly Man, backin up into his house. "You'll be all right."

The little old woman hightailed it home, pushin that wheelbarrow. There was plenty of pine needles around and she and Jackie McPhee sucked on em for quite a while before either of em felt like talkin agin. Then they drunk some clean water outta the jar.

"Well, boy," said the old woman. "I reckon you know when you kin play a trick and when you cain't."

"Yes ma'am," said Jackie McPhee real polite.

"No more rotten eggs on my porch?"

"No ma'am. Cross my heart and hope to spit."

Then the old woman got a twinkle in her eyes.

"I don't spose you could use a thing like this?" she said, lookin at that funny jar of uums.

"Pick me up," said the jar.

"Go ahead," said the little old woman, "take it home, you've earned it."

Well, the little old woman had jest made herself a friend for life. Jackie McPhee grinned a huge gap-toothy grin, picked up that jar, and danced out of them woods, happiest little boy in the world thinkin how he was goin to set his teachers, his folks, and everbody else to sayin UUUUMMMM whenever he pleased.

The little old woman waved good-bye, then tottered off into the kitchen.

It was a shame to lose that batch of blackberry jam, but she had to throw it all out.